YATANDOU

GLORIA WHELAN

paintings by PETER SYLVADA

Tales of the World *from* Sleeping Bear Press

MALI, AFRICA

ACKNOWLEDGMENT

*A special thanks for his help to Lauren Coche,
who at the time I was researching this story,
deployed the multifunctional platform for the
United Nations Development Program.*

G. W.

To Liza Pulitzer Voges

—GLORIA

To my mother with love and admiration

—PETER

Sleeping Bear Press™

310 North Main Street, Suite 300
Chelsea, MI 48118
www.sleepingbearpress.com

Printed and bound in China.

First Edition

10 9 8 7 6 5 4 3 2 1

Library of Congress Cataloging-in-Publication Data on File.
ISBN 10: 1-58536-211-5
ISBN 13: 978-1-58536-211-0

AUTHOR'S NOTE

WHEN I VISITED AFRICA my two strongest impressions were of the beauty of the land and how hard many Africans had to work to take from the land necessities as simple as a drink of water or a dish of porridge. Because their help is so crucial to this work, children are robbed of their childhood and their education. What a satisfaction it was, then, to write the story of Yatandou and the grinding machine (officially known as a multi-functional platform).

With the support of local residents and governments, these multifunctional platforms have been placed in over 350 African villages by the United Nations Development Program. Platforms are owned, operated, and managed by a women's committee appointed by the women's association and the village. To find out more about the multifunctional platforms, go to the program's Web site: www.ptfm.net.

A portion of the author's royalties will be donated to Building with Books™ (BwB). BwB is a not-for-profit organization that engages primarily urban youth through classroom and after-school programs. In the past year students contributed nearly 70,000 hours of service in their communities working with elders, homeless, and young children. Ninety-seven percent of the American high school students BwB has worked with have gone on to college. Students also travel to developing countries to build schools. Of the 192 schools completed, 90 were built in Mali. More than 83,000 children and parents have attended these schools.

Gloria Whelan

Our Mali village lies beneath rocks that stretch like two arms holding us safe. Long ago, the evil emperors came to steal us for slavery. To escape them we lived among the rocks like swallows. Now we are safe on the ground.

When the hot wind blows from the desert I sleep on our roof. The sky is my ceiling and the moon my lantern. Grandmother says it is dangerous on the roof. An evil bird may fly over me and do me harm. I cover myself with my *hawli*, my scarf, so the bird won't see me.

Mother begins her long walk to the water hole in the dark. A rooster's crowing awakens me. Mother is returning. A water jug has had its little journey on her head.

I take my goat to graze. When he was born he was so small and weak he could not nurse. Father said it would be a waste to feed him. I begged Father for the kid and my mother for a little milk.

I call him Sunjata after a famous Mali king. Father says now that the kid has grown into a goat, he is ready to be sold. I don't want to part with him. I rub my cheek against his soft fur. In return, Sunjata nuzzles me.

My brother, Madou, is in a bad mood.
He had to go into the thickets to bring
back one of our goats. I help pull the
krem-krem, the thorns, from his clothes.
In return, he fixes the strap on my
sandals. Madou can fix anything.

Madou and Father will carry soil from
the dried riverbank to make our onion
field larger. The heat in the onion
fields will burn like a thousand fires.
I fill a gourd with water for them.

The desert lives with us. I sweep away the red sand from the courtyard. The sand is everywhere, in my hair, in my eyes, even in my porridge.

My friend Domion sees me sweeping. "Iwè po, iwè po," she greets me. "Yatandou," she says, "we have a new lamb. Come and see it."

Domion is only seven but I am eight and I must pound millet.

"Yemeh ehso, Yatandou," she says. See you later.

My grandmother and my aunts come with their pounding sticks. Their sticks are taller than I am and so heavy I can't lift them. My pounding stick is smaller. It is the stick my mother had when she was a girl.

The women from the village join us. We pound under the shade of a baobab tree. The baobab trees have names. This tree is called, "Biting Fruit." When you bite into the fruit, it bites back. To get enough millet meal for one day's food, we must pound the kernels for three hours. My arms and back hurt.

While I pound I dream about a new pair of earrings. I think
of what it would be like to go to school and learn book secrets
like my brother did. I watch a fish eagle fly where it wants to.

The women talk of bringing to the village something that will
eat the millet kernels and spit out meal.

My pounding stick grows heavier and heavier. I ask Mother,
"How soon will the thing that chews up the millet come to
our village?"

"Not until the women in our village have enough money,"
she says.

Mother sells her onion balls,
Grandmother her water jars.

I wish I had something to sell.
I remember Sunjata, but I think
of his soft fur against my cheek.

When our baskets are filled with millet
meal Mother begins to pound the
onions. I help her make the pulp into
balls for sauce. We carry the balls up to
the roof to dry. Our whole house has a
fine onion smell.

Mother and I go in search of firewood for cooking. The hot sun sends our shadows with us. I try to walk in Mother's shadow. There is danger in being far from the village. Bad spirits, *jinu*, hide in the bush. They will steal a child and put another child in that child's place.

We pile the firewood upon our heads. Even with a folded head cloth, my branches keep slipping off. Mother adds some of my branches to her pile.

Mother makes another journey to the well. Darkness comes before she returns. Father is angry because no dinner has been prepared.

Mother says, "With the pounding and the fetching of the water and the getting of the firewood, there was no time to prepare a dinner."

I am not angry but I am hungry.

On market day I tie on my *pagne*, my skirt, which Grandmother has dyed a bright blue. My blouse is yellow with a ruffle around the collar. Mother ties a red *hawli* on her head. She takes a basket of onion balls to sell.

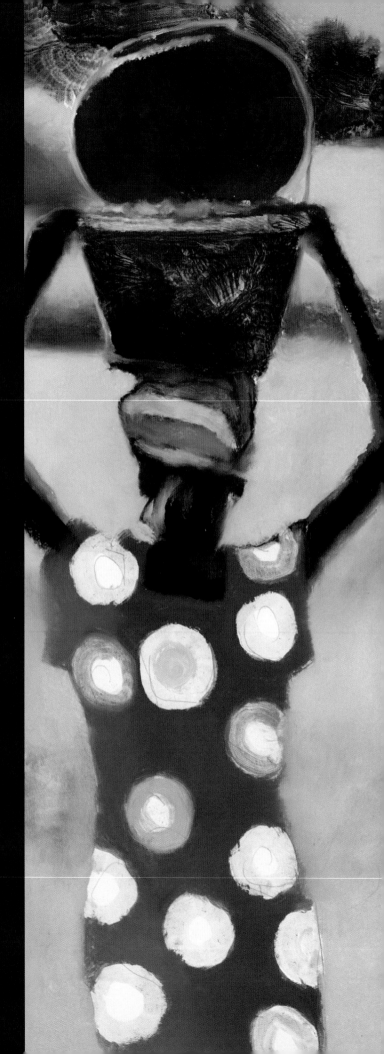

I put a rope around Sunjata so I can lead him to the market.

Each market stall has a different colored awning. One stall is heaped with red tomatoes and green peppers. There are baskets of *niebe*, each bean with a little black eye that looks at you. Chickens flap their wings, raising dust. Hawkers sell little bundles of green *sèngè* leaves to feed to the goats.

A *griot*, a wandering singer, plays his lute and sings the story of King Sunjata. The medicine man holds up a snake in one hand and a dried bird with bright feathers in the other hand.

I sell Sunjata to an old woman for
a good price. First I make her promise
not to eat him.

"Oh, no," the woman says, "he is a
fine goat. He will be used to help in
the making of more goats."

I give the money to Mother. "Now can
we put the pounding sticks away?" I ask.

"Soon," she says.

☰☷

I carry home the empty rope.

One morning Madou hurries into the courtyard.

"Ça va? What is happening?" my father asks. The French once held our country of Mali in their hands. When they went away, some of their words were left behind.

Madou says, "A truck was seen coming from Bandiagara with a big package for our village."

We all run to see the truck. On the back of the truck is a big hump hidden beneath a heavy cloth. The name of our country, Mali, comes from the word hippopotamus. I wonder if the package is one of the great beasts.

A disappointment! It is only a contraption made of wheels and strangely shaped pails joined by metal snakes. Madou with his clever hands helps to put the contraption together.

The man says, "Who will be the first to give me their millet to grind? The cost for the grinding will be fifty francs."

Mother steps forward and hands the man a basket of millet and fifty francs. The price of two mangoes!

The millet goes in and in less time than it would take Mother to wind her *hawli* around her head, out comes the meal. Mother can sell the meal for a hundred francs.

The man says, "The women must write down who puts the millet into the machine and how much they pay."

The women can't write but they say, "We will find someone to teach us."

A woman comes from the city. She is one of us but she is not one of us. She wears *bantalons*, pants, instead of a dress or a *pagne*. She teaches us girls as well as the women.

All the words I said to Domion used to disappear with the saying. Now I can write a word down and give it to her. She can write a word down and give it to me. How strange it is to see that our words have a face!

Instead of the sound of the pounding sticks there is only the whir and rumble of the contraption. With each grinding, it makes money. When there is enough money, the contraption will bring water out of the ground and light to our village.

Father complains, "If the women are idle it will make trouble."

Madou climbs the rocks and brings home a bag of bats from the caves. Mother makes Father's favorite bat stew for dinner. Father smiles and says nothing more about idleness.

I have learned to write my name. I take my pencil and spell out YATANDOU on my pounding stick. When I have a little girl I will show the stick to her. I will tell her how I raised Sunjata and sold him and how that helped to bring the contraption to our village.

She will show the pounding stick to her daughter, who will never have to use it.